CAPTAIN BOB
Takes Flight

by RONI SCHOTTER
Illustrated by JOE CEPEDA

An Anne Schwartz Book
Atheneum Books for Young Readers
NEW YORK   LONDON   TORONTO   SYDNEY   SINGAPORE

He was Captain Bob,
and he was the finest,
fiercest flyer that ever flew
the cloud-cluttered skies.

He feared no one, not even the curly-headed Control Tower who called out his orders: **"Clear the runway!"**

"I do the job *my* way," Bob bravely called back, "the fun way."

He needed no help
from any ground crew
for his mission. With
his Sky Scarf 'round
his neck, Wind Socks
on his feet, and Fog
Goggles over his eyes,
he packed his flight bag
chock-a-block full
of flying gear.

Then, climbing into his cushioned cockpit,
Bob placed his headphones over his ears.
He was ready for takeoff.

"Up and away, I say," he commanded, pulling up on his Throttle Bottle. "Back in an hour, Control Tower."

It was a crowded sky, but Bob steered clear of danger. He flew a careful course over unidentified low-lying objects, scooping them up in his Supersonic Rescue Cup.

Then he dropped them,
one by one, where they belonged.

"I'm Captain Bob, the Fly Boy!" Bob shouted. "Here we go loopty-loo!"

He pressed his
Automatic Booster
Control Button, turned,
and did three perfect head-
and-tail spins. Now feeling
dizzy, he set his flight path for
the wild blue yonder where he
could rest and idle-a-while.

Humming along with
his engine, Bob took
his harmonica from his
instrument panel, then
played an airy tune, as
he zoomed up, toward
the light of the moon.

High above, where a curtain of clouds floated free, Bob reached into an air pocket and took out his flight pad and pencil. "Time for some sky writing," he announced.

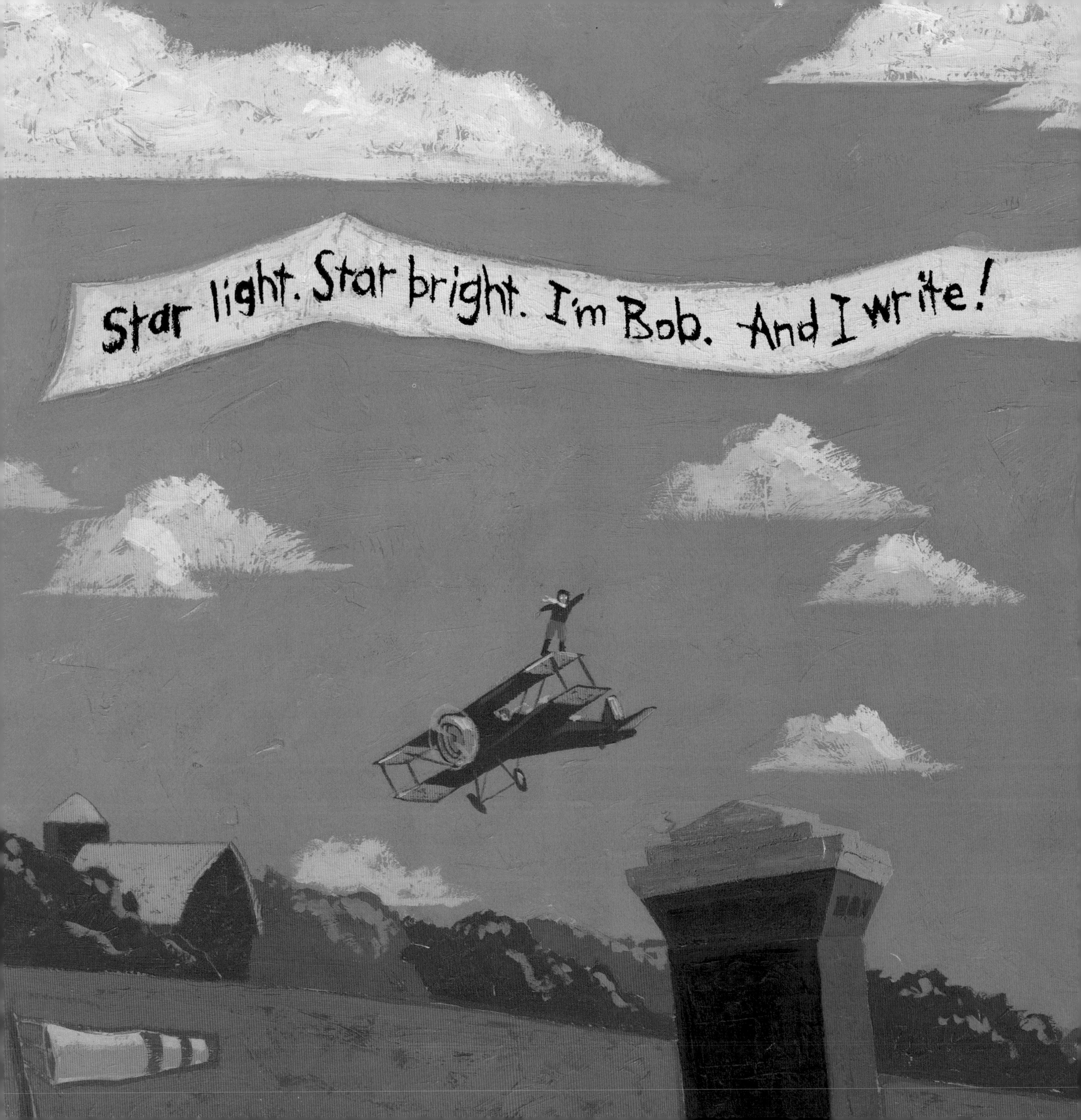
Star light. Star bright. I'm Bob. And I write!

And way up there, beyond the birds, in large lovely letters, Bob wrote his words: "Star light. Star bright. I'm Bob. And I write!"

Now hovering near a Sky Hook,
Bob hitched up to read
his favorite flying book.

But suddenly a blast of southerly, strangely motherly wind blew in. . . . The cockpit *shook*. Bob dropped his book.

"Captain Bob to Control Tower," he called over the airwaves. "Come in!"

"Control Tower to Captain Bob," came the reply. "Time to land. Is the runway clear?"

"Captain Bob, ace pilot, here. Mission done. All clear!"

Bob wiped some stardust from his wings with his Sky Scarf, then raised his flaps. Pushing down on his Throttle Bottle, he waved good-bye to the sky and pointed his nose toward the Motherland.

It was lunchtime and Bob was a tired, hungry captain. Turning on his landing lights, he glided down through a pea-soup-hard-to-see-soup fog.

How that Control Tower greeted him on his return! She kissed him, told him how she had missed him. Then she gave him his lunch. And can you guess why? Do you have any doubt?

Because he was Captain Bob,
the finest, fiercest Fly Boy.
Over and out!

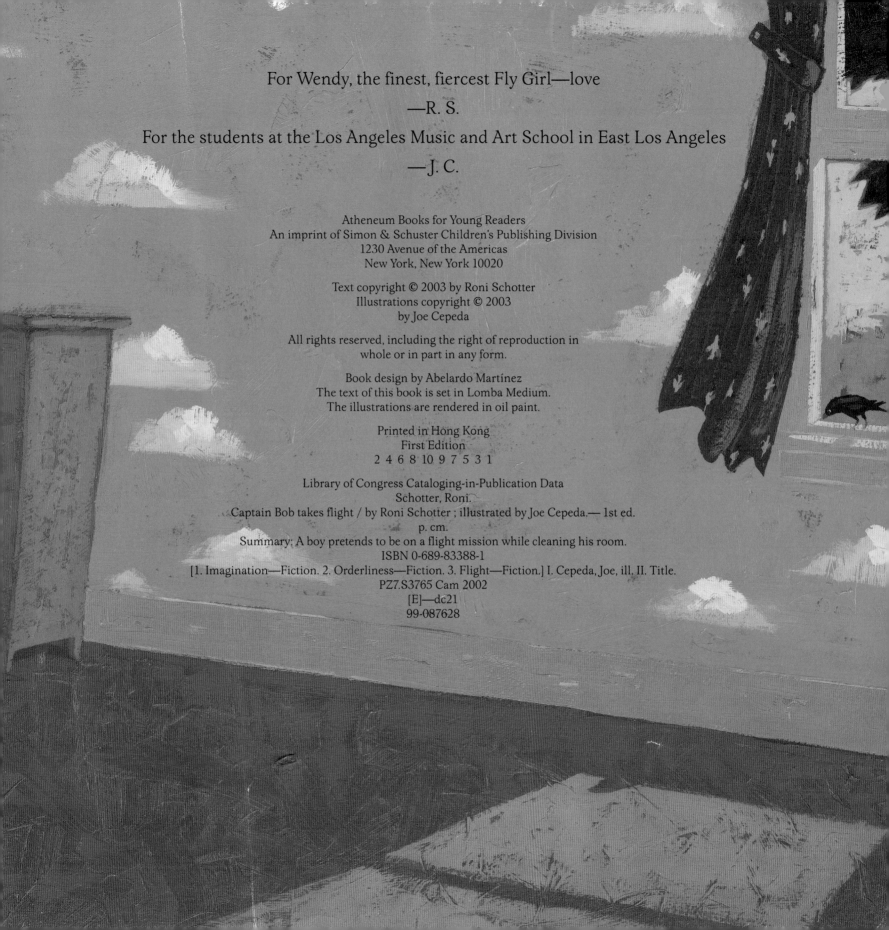

For Wendy, the finest, fiercest Fly Girl—love
—R. S.

For the students at the Los Angeles Music and Art School in East Los Angeles
—J. C.

Atheneum Books for Young Readers
An imprint of Simon & Schuster Children's Publishing Division
1230 Avenue of the Americas
New York, New York 10020

Book design by Abelardo Martínez
The text of this book is set in Lomba Medium.
The illustrations are rendered in oil paint.

Printed in Hong Kong
First Edition
2 4 6 8 10 9 7 5 3 1

Library of Congress Cataloging-in-Publication Data
Schotter, Roni.
Captain Bob takes flight / by Roni Schotter ; illustrated by Joe Cepeda.— 1st ed.
p. cm.
Summary: A boy pretends to be on a flight mission while cleaning his room.
ISBN 0-689-83388-1
[1. Imagination—Fiction. 2. Orderliness—Fiction. 3. Flight—Fiction.] I. Cepeda, Joe, ill. II. Title.
PZ7.S3765 Cam 2002
[E]—dc21
99-087628